To the student reading this book...

you are very special and extraordinary!

Silly the Seed

A portion of proceeds from the sale of Silly the Seed will be donated to First Book, a nonprofit organization that provides new books for children in need. Learn more about their work at www.firstbook.org

Color, image editing, and book design by El Yves Margarita

Silly the Seed
Copyright © 2011 by Scott Sussman
Printed in China by Kings Time Printing Press, Ltd.
All rights reserved.
ISBN 978-0-9829506-0-9
Library of Congress Catalog Number: 2010915638

The display type is set in Akbar, a typeface created and designed
by Jon Bernhardt, and is used with his permission.

Third Printing, June 2016

www.octopusinkpress.com

Silly the Seed

OCTOPUS INK
PRESS

This is the story
of Silly the Seed.

His parents named him Silly
because he's silly indeed.
(This is his silly face.)

Silly was happy.
Yes, that was true.
Silly's a special seed
and that much he knew.

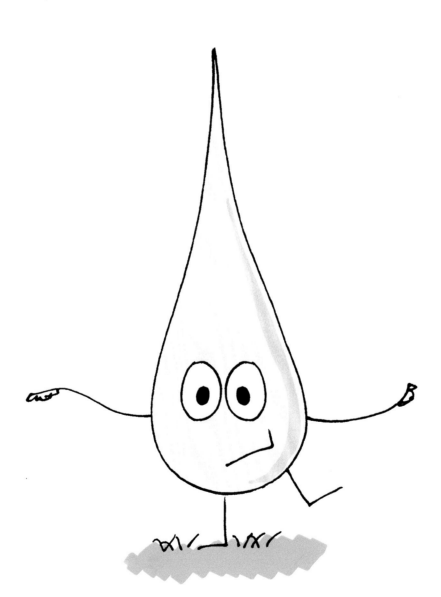

So with a smile on his face
Silly went on his way
and walked along thinking
about the wonderful day.
(There's the silly face again.)

Just then Silly saw
under a rock in the park...

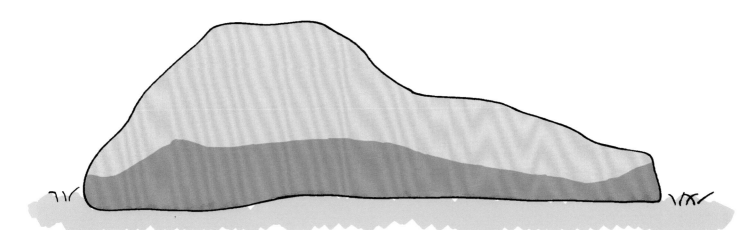

...a wiggly worm
caught in the dark.

Silly went to help
(he knew what to do)
he lifted the rock
and let the sunshine through.

The worm looked at Silly
as if to say,
"Thanks for the help!"
Then he wiggled away.

Thanksforthehelp

So with a smile on his face
Silly went on his way
and walked along thinking
about the wonderful day.
(He loves to do the silly face.)

Then Silly saw
in the trunk of a tree...

...a Bunuga bug
stuck by a knee.

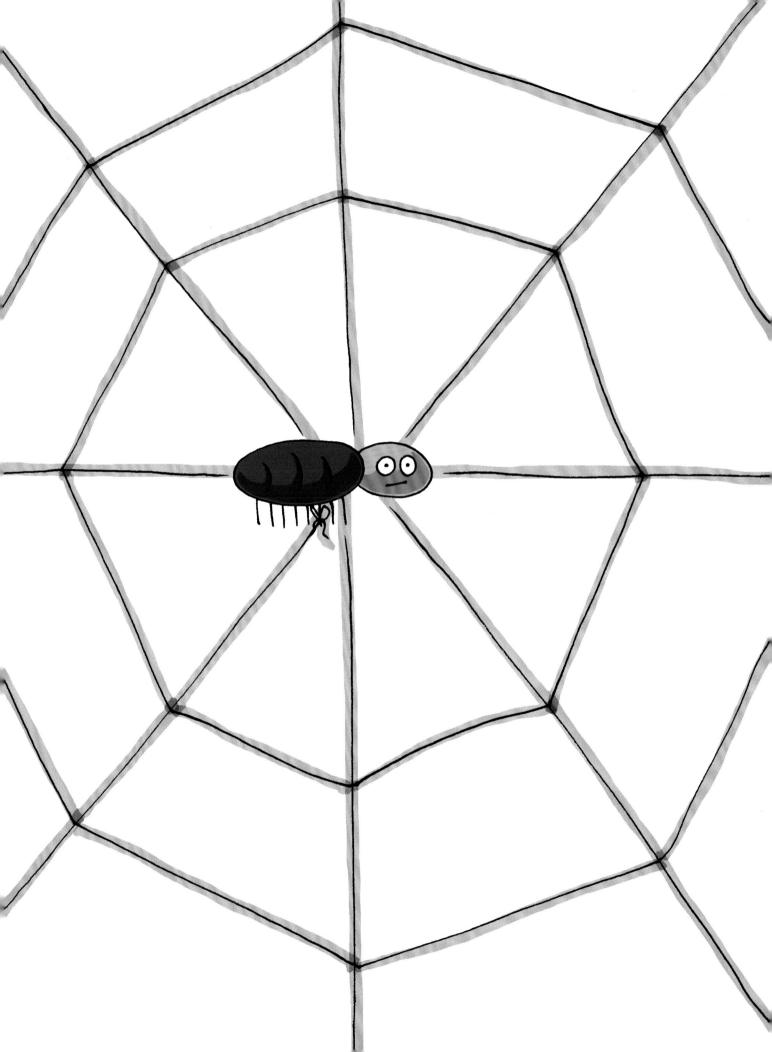

Silly went to the tree
(to help the bug)
and unstuck his knee
with a twist and a tug.

The bug looked at Silly
as if to say,
"Gee, thanks a lot!"
Then he hopped away.

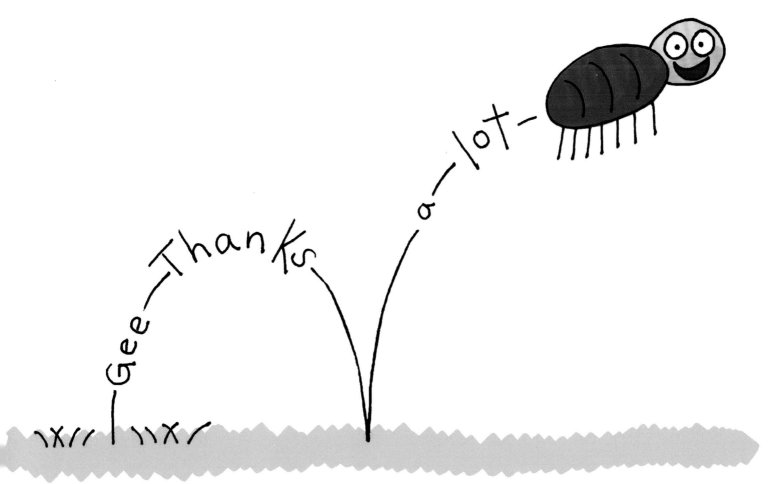

So with a smile on his face
Silly went on his way
and walked along thinking
about the wonderful day.
(He's so silly.)

But then Silly fell
in a hole in the ground
and waited there hoping
soon to be found.

That's when Silly saw
in a part of the sky
a lone cloud watching
with a close-watching eye.

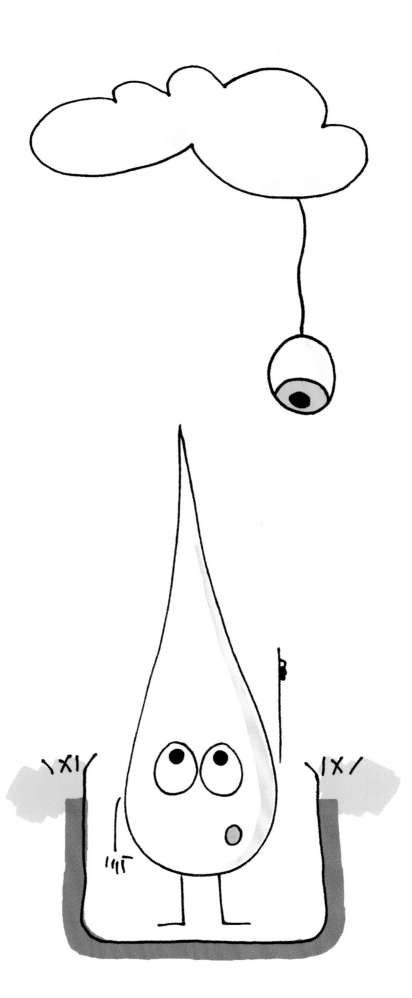

the cloud looked at Silly
as if to say,
"You are a special seed!"
Then it turned gray.

In the flash of a smile
and the wink of an eye,
the cloud rained on Silly
and left him less dry.

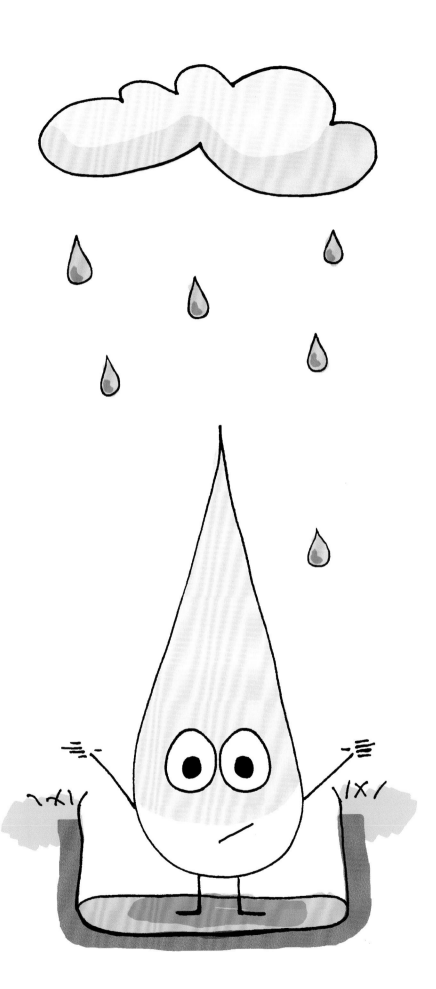

With a kick and a push
and under an hour...

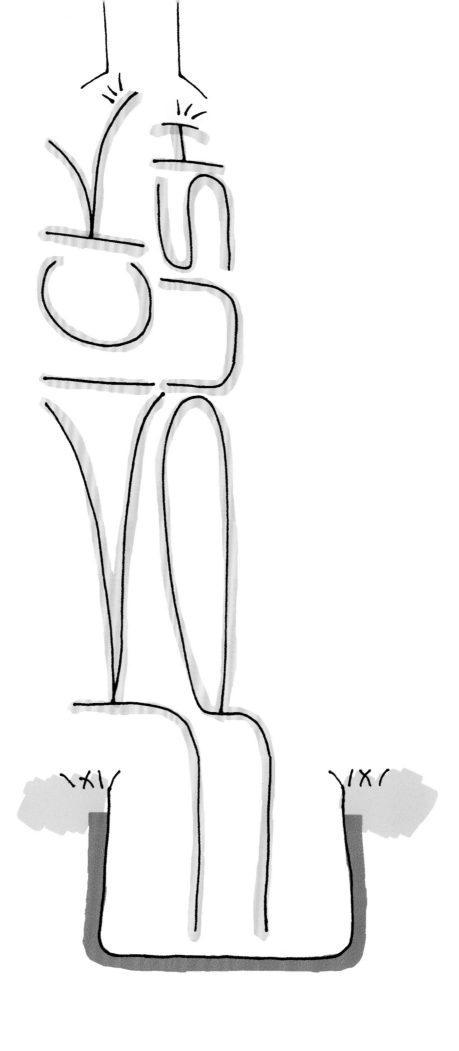

...Silly became
a beautiful flower.

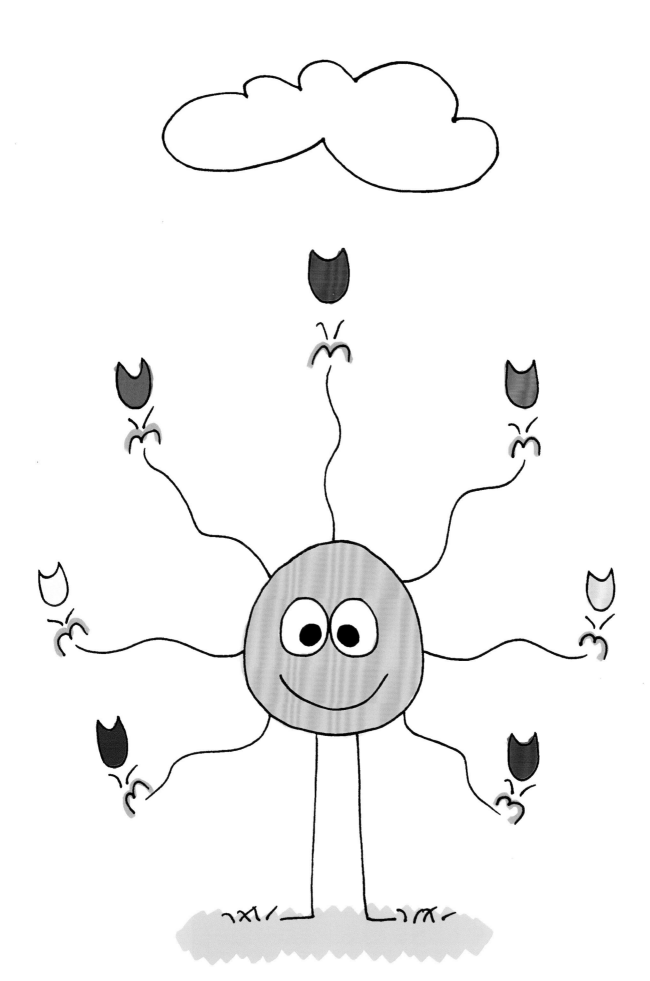

With a smile on his face
as Silly already knew
he is a special seed
like you and me too.
(What a silly face!)

Also from
OCTOPUS INK PRESS

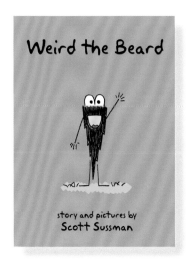

Weird the Beard

Weird the Beard is the amusing journey of a beard that makes friends by cracking jokes. But the joke's on Weird when he tries to befriend a suspicious-looking razor. Needless to say, he will never be the same.

Lerky the Handturkey

Lerky the Handturkey is the inspiring story of a handturkey whose wise words encourage others to see the bright side. It's the companion to Silly the Seed and Weird the Beard, a wacky tale of friendship and optimism.

Fred and the Monster
2015 Silver Medal Winner - Independent Publisher Awards

Fred is afraid of the dark. So is the monster under his bed. One night, Fred's mom does the unthinkable... she turns off the light! Stricken with terror, Fred and the monster must rely on each other for the courage to face their worst fear.

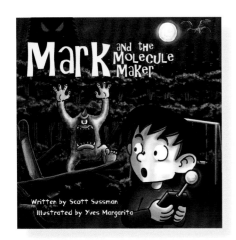

Mark and the Molecule Maker

When Mark enters his father's laboratory and finds the Molecule Maker, he flips the switch and makes a monster. Things go from bad to worse when the creature escapes and Mark races against the sunrise to right the wrong.

Mark and the Molecule Maker 2: The Lightning Jungle

The adventure continues with book two of the Mark and the Molecule Maker trilogy. When the Molecule Maker malfunctions, creating a bunch of mischievous creatures that kidnap Mark's father, Mark races into the lightning jungle on an amazing rescue mission. But will he arrive before it's too late?

Mark and the Molecule Maker 3: The Underground Mountain

In the thrilling conclusion to the Mark and the Molecule Maker trilogy, the chase is on when a cunning monster steals the Molecule Maker. In a desperate attempt to retrieve the extraordinary invention, Mark and his father must risk their lives on the treacherous underground mountain, where danger lurks behind every boulder and hides inside every hole.

The Shining Adventures of Shelpa McStorm

The trip of a lifetime on the most exclusive vacation planet in the universe! Shelpa McStorm has barely set foot in the crystal blue ocean of Panacea when he is thrust into a wild adventure through enchanted forests and forbidden lands. Along the way he encounters a hitchhiking hat, a cornball king, a wacko meatball, and a host of other crazy characters. Shelpa's life is about to take an incredible turn. Although he thinks he is racing to rescue a friendly flower, his real quest is to save himself.

Chapter book, paperback, 208 pages

Visit our website at

www.octopusinkpress.com

for updates and information regarding future publications.